Eliza's Kindergarten Pet

by Alice B. McGinty

illustrated by Nancy Speir

MARSHALL CAVENDISH CHILDREN

Marshall Cavendish Corporation, 99 White Plains Road, Tarrytown, NY 10591
www.marshallcavendish.us/kids

Library of Congress Cataloging-in-Publication Data

McGinty, Alice B.
Eliza's kindergarten pet / by Alice B. McGinty ;
illustrated by Nancy Speir. —1st ed.
p. cm.
Summary: When the kindergarten classroom gets a pet guinea pig Eliza
is afraid, but when the guinea pig gets lost, Eliza helps find her.
ISBN 978-0-7614-5702-2
[1. Guinea pigs—Fiction. 2. Fear—Fiction. 3. Lost and found
possessions—Fiction. 4. Kindergarten—Fiction. 5. Schools—Fiction.]
I. Speir, Nancy, ill. II. Title.
PZ7.M16777El 2010
[E]—dc22
2009046008

The illustrations are rendered in arcylic on illustration board.
Book design by Becky Terhune
Editor: Margery Cuyler
Printed in Malaysia (T)
First edition
1 3 5 6 4 2

 **Marshall Cavendish**
Children

To my niece, Emily
—A. B. M.

For Gus
—N. S.

When Miss Summer brought Cookie to Kindergarten for the first time, Eliza frowned.

"She's wiggly and she squeals," Eliza said. "She has a mouth with teeth."

"So do all guinea pigs," said Miss Summer. "What do you think we should call her?"

"Cookie!" said Eliza's friend Ruth. "Her spots look like chocolate chips."

A cookie with teeth? Eliza thought. She knew that people ate chocolate chip cookies. Did chocolate chip cookies ever eat people?

At Monday Meeting, Miss Summer told the class that everybody would take turns being Kindergarten Cookie Keeper.

"Cookie needs food.
Cookie needs water.
Cookie needs treats.
And Cookie needs love,"
said Miss Summer.

Eliza turned to Ruth.
"I do not want to be Cookie Keeper," she said.
"I do not want to visit Cookie's side of the room.
I will find a job on my side of the room."

Later that day, Ruth took the first turn as Kindergarten Cookie Keeper.

From across the room, Eliza watched Ruth fill Cookie's water bowl, pour food into Cookie's food bowl, and give Cookie a treat. When Ruth picked up Cookie to pet her, Eliza climbed on top of her desk.

What if the wiggly Cookie, the Cookie with teeth, escaped?

It felt safer to be out of the way.

On Tuesday, Sam took his turn as Cookie Keeper.
He filled the water bowl and the food bowl.
Then he held out chunks of carrot for Cookie.
When Cookie nibbled them, Sam giggled.

FOOD

On the other side of the room, Eliza frowned.

"What if Cookie nibbles a finger instead of a treat?" she asked Ruth.
    "Cookie eats carrots, not fingers," said Ruth.

On Wednesday, Eliza stood close to the door
as she watched Michelle take care of Cookie.

It felt much safer near the door. After all, if wiggly
Cookie, Cookie with teeth, escaped, she could go
anywhere — even to Eliza's side of the room.

On Thursday, that is exactly what happened. Eric was holding Cookie on his lap when he tipped his chair back — too far! The chair fell over, Eric landed on the floor, and Cookie skittered toward Eliza's side of the room.

Before Eliza could run into the hall . . .

Cookie disappeared!

Everyone, except Eliza,
searched for Cookie.

Even Ms. Manchester, the custodian, helped.
Cookie was not behind the cabinets.
She was not under the bookshelves.
She was not in the toy box.

When the bell rang to go home, there was no sign of Cookie anywhere.

On Friday, when Eliza got to school,
there was still no Cookie.
"Where do you think she is?" asked Eliza.
"Don't worry," said Miss Summer.
"I'm sure Cookie will turn up soon."

"Me, worried?" said Eliza.

FOOD

But Eliza did feel worried.

All morning, she could not work.
She could not play.
She could only think of Cookie.

Where was Cookie?

When the class went to lunch,
there was still no sign of Cookie.

Eliza sat down and took a bite of her sandwich.
Then she heard a scuffle. There, in the corner,
stood Ms. Manchester, the custodian, pushing her
broom at a blob. A blob with dark brown spots.
"Cookie!" Eliza yelled. She ran over.

"Hold on," said Ms. Manchester.
"She might bite. I'll push her into
a box with the broom."

Push Cookie into a box with a broom?
Eliza thought.

Eliza looked at Cookie huddled in the corner.

Cookie looked scared.

Cookie would not like being pushed into a box with a broom.

"Wait," Eliza said. "I'll help." She walked to the corner.
"It's okay," Eliza said to Cookie. She gently scooped her
up and held her close. She could feel Cookie trembling.
"You're okay," said Eliza, though she was trembling, too.

Eliza carried Cookie slowly back to the classroom.

"Look who I found," she said to Miss Summer.

"Welcome back, Cookie," said Miss Summer. "Where have you been?"

"In the cafeteria," the other kids said. "Eliza rescued her!"

Eliza sat down with Cookie on her lap. She began to pet her. Cookie stopped trembling and began to purr.

After a while, Eliza put Cookie in her cage.
She filled Cookie's water bowl, poured new food,
and held out some bits of carrot.

Cookie nibbled them and Eliza giggled.
Cookie's nibbles did tickle after all.

"Do you know what we need today?" said Miss Summer.

"A Cookie Keeper," said Eliza. "That's me!"

FOOD